For Nia Lewis and June Henley who met in the sun ~ CH

Papers used by Scholastic Children's Books
are made from wood grown
in sustainable forests.

First published in 2011 by Scholastic Children's Books, Euston House, 24 Eversholt Street, London NW1 1DE
a division of Scholastic Ltd, www.scholastic.co.uk
London ~ New York ~ Toronto ~ Sydney ~ Auckland ~ Mexico City ~ New Delhi ~ Hong Kong
Text and illustrations copyright © 2011 Claire Henley
PB ISBN 978 1407 11541 2
All rights reserved. Printed in Singapore
1 3 5 7 9 10 8 6 4 2
The moral rights of Claire Henley have been asserted.

Bella
the Brave
Fairy

Claire Henley

SCHOLASTIC

Deep in the woods, beneath the shady
leaves and soft petals was a secret place
re the fairies lived.

Bella Blossom was the smallest fairy of all.
When her friends grew glorious wings,
Bella grew little fluttery buds, but they
were too tiny for flying.

She got around by climbing and jumping instead of whizzing and whooshing. Bella did her best to stay cheerful, but she desperately longed to join in with the others.

Bella's friends wanted to help.

"Just bend your knees
and JUMP!"
smiled Lily Leaf.

"Flap your
wings as hard
as you can,"
said Daisy Dew.

"Shout, One, Two, Three,
WHEEEE..."
squealed Poppy Pink.

Bella tried everything,
but it was no good. Her feet
stayed firmly on the ground.

Luckily there were plenty of things to do in the fairy village that didn't involve flying.

Bella liked reading stories to the littlest fairies...

...and boating on the lake.

But best of all, she loved playing games among the
flowers with her friends. There was one fairy,
however, who wasn't as much fun as all the rest.

Delphine Dazzle had the finest
pair of wings and could fly higher
and faster than any other fairy in
the village.

When she wasn't boasting loudly and making people feel silly, she liked to play cruel tricks on some of the other fairies. Because of this they all called her Mean Delphine.

Mean Delphine was
especially mean to Bella.
"If you can't fly, you'll never
be good at anything!" she sneered.

"Look at me, Bella!"

called Mean Delphine.

"Bet you can't do this!"

"Show-off," muttered Daisy Dew.
"Just ignore her, Bella."
But Bella couldn't.
   "Delphine's right,"
she said to herself.
"I'm no good at **anything**."

One night, Bella couldn't sleep.
She tiptoed quietly to the lakeside for a drink.
On the way she tried a few hops and jumps,
hoping secretly for a miracle.

Suddenly there was a rush of air and a flutter of wings as Mean Delphine soared above Bella's head.

"What ARE you doing, funny Bella?

Haven't you given up trying to fly? You'll NEVER manage it with those teeny weenie wings!"

Bella blushed and started to hurry back to bed, wishing Delphine had not seen her hopeful hops and jumps.

Suddenly there was a piercing shriek.
Bella peered into the darkness and saw
something high above the lake that made
her heart thump loudly.

There, trapped in the centre of an enormous spider's web, was Mean Delphine.

"Help!" she squealed. "My wings are tangled – I can't move!"

There was a pinging sound as the old web began to sag and break.

"Hurry, Bella!" cried Delphine. "Please DO something!"

Bella sprang to the nearest bulrush and climbed as
fast as she could to the top. She had never been
so far off the ground.

"I'm coming,
Delphine!" she
called bravely.

At last Bella reached Delphine
and held out a shaky arm.

"Grab my hand, Delphine!" she called.

"Come on, you can do it!"

Just as Delphine clasped Bella's hand,
there was another loud ping, and the
old web collapsed.

The two fairies clung to each other as the bulrush swung madly to and fro.

"I'm so sorry," sobbed Delphine, hugging Bella tightly.

"I've been so mean to you, and all the time you've been the bravest and strongest of us all."

All the commotion had awakened the other fairies. When Delphine and Bella reached the ground, the cheer was so loud that even you or I might have heard it.

"You're so clever, Bella," said Daisy Dew.
"We're really proud of you," grinned Lily Leaf.
"You're a heroine!" squealed Poppy Pink.

Bella smiled as a warm glow spread inside her.
"Perhaps," she thought to herself, "I might be
quite good at something after all."

The End